Snow-White And Rose-Red

&

The Frog Prince

Snow-White And Rose-Red & The Frog Prince

Fairytales Retold
Double Edition

Avril Sabine

Cracked Acorn Productions
Australia

Snow-White And Rose-Red & The Frog Prince

Fairytales Retold Double Edition

Published by

Cracked Acorn Productions

PO Box 1365

Gympie, Queensland 4570

Australia

978-1-925131-93-2 (Large Type Print)

Genre: Fairytales Retold Short Story

Snow-White And Rose-Red

★

The Frog Prince

Snow-White
And
Rose-Red

Snow-White and Rose-Red live with their widowed mother in a cottage in the middle of a forest. One winter's night a bear knocks on their door wanting to come in and warm himself at their fire.

*

People have been telling stories since the beginning of time. Fairytales, folklore, myths and legends are among some of the stories that have been told over and over through the centuries. The basic story remains the same, but each storyteller adds their own style, sometimes adding something unique to the tale.

*

This story was written by an Australian author using Australian spelling.

Snow-White And Rose-Red

Snow brushed strands of her pale blond hair back from her face, bending down to pick up another piece of firewood. She added it to the bundle she carried on her back before turning to her younger sister. "We should turn for home soon. Tonight will probably bring our first snow for this winter."

Rose groaned. "But we haven't gotten around to digging up all the potatoes from the vegetable patch."

Like her sister, her long hair hung down her back in a single plait. She had a shawl draped around her head, hiding most of her red hair from view and also carried a bundle of firewood.

"They'll keep. We'll dig them up when we need them." Snow again bent for more firewood, the bundle she carried growing heavier and more awkward.

"They're so much harder to dig up once it snows. And I haven't finished spinning enough wool to knit a new pair of gloves." Rose held out a hand in front of her, the grey gloves worn through in places. "They're beyond darning."

Snow could feel every hole in her own gloves. "You're only annoyed because the weather will keep you inside and there'll be no more exploring the forest until spring."

Rose grabbed a fallen branch. "If only we had the money for warm clothes, then I'd spend all year exploring the forest." She dragged the branch behind her.

The wind picked up and Snow shivered, wishing she too had a shawl, even if it was threadbare like her sister's. Maybe this year they'd be able to spin enough wool to not only knit new gloves for each of them, but also sell some at the market come spring. To sell enough to afford a length of cloth to make all of them new clothes. Picking up one last piece of firewood, Snow changed directions. "Let's go home." She couldn't help sighing at the thought of all the work that still awaited them at home.

Rose reached for her sister's hand. "It's all right, Snow. I don't really mind winter. Don't be so sad."

Snow smiled. "I was thinking of everything we still have to do when we get home, that's all."

Rose squeezed Snow's hand. "If you build up the fire and put the brass kettle on to boil, I'll prepare the vegetables for the stew."

"Thank you, Rose." This time it was Snow who squeezed her sister's hand and Rose who smiled.

They walked home in silence, both shivering by the time they reached the cottage, dropping their firewood in the lean-to at the side of their home. Rose hurried inside, calling a greeting to their mother, Anna. Snow paused at the front door to look at the two rose bushes, one planted on either side of the door.

She reached out and ran a finger down a branch of the one on her left, careful to avoid the thorns. Her mother had planted it seventeen years ago on the day she'd been born, sending her husband to the shepherd's wife for a cutting from one of her rose bushes. Anna had told her many times over the years that her white blond hair had reminded her of a snow-white rose. When her sister had arrived two years after her, with red hair, her mother had planted the second bush. Its flower was a dark red.

"Snow-White, come inside and close the door. You're letting the cold in," Anna called out.

With one last glance at the darkening sky, Snow hurried inside, closing the door behind her. "I think it'll snow tonight." She crossed the room to the fire. Stirring it up, she added more wood.

Near the fire a motherless lamb

rested, while a white dove Snow had rescued the previous year, sat on a perch. There was a table with two chairs, the third wooden chair being used by Anna who sat not far from the fire, her spindle in one hand, a basket of wool on the floor beside her. At one end of the cottage was Anna's bed, covered by the quilt she'd sewn before she'd left her own mother's house. At the other end were two narrow beds, each with a quilt Anna had made while she'd been pregnant with her daughters. The quilts covered each bed, the sides brushing against the timber floor, the different coloured pieces long since faded. There was a chest at the foot of Anna's bed with three more quilts, folded and stored with herbs, for her children who hadn't lived.

Anna nodded. "All the signs point to a hard winter ahead."

Rose sat at the table, dicing vegetables on its scarred wooden surface. "As long as it's not a long winter, I don't care."

"It will be what it needs to be, Rose-Red. Your complaining about it won't make it any shorter," Anna said.

After checking there was enough water in the brass kettle, Snow hung it on the hook over the fire, her reflection showing in the shiny surface. She turned to Anna. "Will you read to us tonight?"

Rose pushed the vegetables into a wooden bowl, rising from the table. "Please, Mother? You said you'd read us more from father's book when the days grew shorter. They've been short for weeks." She tipped the vegetables into the kettle that was starting to bubble.

"For a little while. We haven't the candles to waste." Anna continued to spin wool.

"I'll get it." Snow hurried towards her mother's end of the cottage, taking the large book off a shelf, and picking up the spectacles that sat beside it. She cradled the book against her chest as she returned to her mother's side. The book was all that was left of the father she barely recalled.

After handing the book and spectacles to her mother, Snow bolted the front door and brought the chairs to the fire, while Rose gathered the wool and spindles. Putting aside her own spindle, Anna put on her spectacles and opened the book. She cleared her throat then began to read.

The rhythm of her mother's voice blended with the rhythm of the spindle and Snow smiled slightly as she listened, her hands continuing to keep the spindle in motion. The wind picked up, causing the shutters to rattle lightly. The sound of the fire crackling and the stew bubbling gently were the only other sounds in the room other than her mother's voice.

The smell of stew filled the room and Snow continued to put off serving the meal, knowing her mother would stop reading the moment she rose from her seat. A banging at the door, brought Anna's voice to a halt and the three of them turned towards it.

"Who would be crazy enough to be out in this weather?" Rose asked.

"Whatever poor traveller it is will

be half frozen," Anna said. "Go see who it is, Rose-Red. Snow-White, our dinner smells like it's well past ready to be served. Put out a bowl for our visitor too."

Snow put aside her spindle and gathered wooden bowls from the shelf near the fire, setting them on the table while Rose walked towards the door. Taking the metal ladle from the shelf and a wooden spoon for each bowl, Snow put the spoons on the table and grabbing a folded cloth, headed for the fire.

A gust of wind tore through the cottage as Rose opened the door and screamed. Still clutching the ladle and folded cloth, her heart racing, Snow spun to face the door. Her breath stopped in her throat at the sight of the large black bear framed in the doorway, snow swirling around him and settling on the cottage floor.

Anna hurried towards the door as Rose backed away from it. Snow dashed across the room, her shoulder colliding with the far wall since she could not take her gaze from the bear. Calling for her sister, she dropped the ladle as she held out a hand for her.

"I mean you no harm. I only want to warm myself at your fire," the bear said.

Rose stopped retreating, Snow remained frozen by her mother's bed, her hand still outstretched and Anna took another step forward.

"Oh you poor bear. Come in, come in. Warm yourself by our fire." Anna gestured towards the fire. The bear ambled inside and she closed the door again, throwing the bolt home. "Come girls, no need to be afraid. He means us no harm. Dish out the meal, Snow-White."

Snow came hesitantly forward, picking up the ladle and dusting it off, keeping a wary eye on the bear. She took the kettle from the fire and filled the bowls with stew. Both her and her sister had brought home animals from the forest over the years. Hurt or sick animals in need of care, but never a bear. Never an animal with sharp white teeth that was large enough to eat them.

With trembling hands, she took the bowl of stew to the bear who had laid down in front of the fire. "Here." There was a tremble in her voice as she placed the bowl in front of him.

"I wish you no harm, Snow-White," the bear rumbled.

Snow took a step back, startled at hearing her name spoken in such a deep voice. "I… I hope you enjoy the stew." She could think of nothing else to say. What did you talk about with a bear? The only other words that came to mind were, 'please don't eat me,' and it was a thought she didn't want to put into his mind if it wasn't already there.

"Thank you for sharing your meal with me." The bear lowered his head and began to lap up the stew.

Snow continued to back away until she collided with her chair that was not far from the fire. Turning, she grabbed the chair and retreated to the table where her sister and mother were already sitting. Adding more water to the kettle from the jug, sitting on a side table near the kitchen shelf, Snow returned it to the fire. She hung it at the side to keep it warm, before she sat at the table.

The meal was silent. Snow and Rose both sending frequent glances towards the bear and sharing equally frequent looks with each other. When the meal was ended, Snow gathered up the dishes and washed them in a bowl of water kept on the side table.

"Rose-Red, grab a cloth and mop up the floor around the bear. The snow in his fur is melting and creating puddles," Anna ordered.

Rose sent Snow a pleading look and Snow dried her hands on her skirt. "If you want to tip the dishwater outside, I'll mop the floor." She tried to keep the fear from her voice, but wasn't certain she had succeeded. Grabbing a worn cloth, she slowly crossed the room. Behind her she felt a gust of wind fill the cottage as her sister tossed out the water. The door closed again, shutting out the wind.

Snow knelt beside the bear, who had finished his meal and had his eyes closed. When she started to mop the floor, he raised his head to stare at her with his dark brown eyes. She fought against the urge to flee. Her hands stilled.

"If you knock the snow from my fur I will dry quicker and leave less puddles on the floor."

Snow could only nod. It took an age before she could let go of the cloth and reach out to knock the dusting of snow from his fur. His coat was cold and coarse and after a few minutes, she grew less fearful when he remained still. When the job was done and the floor mopped, Snow spread the cloth out near the fire to dry.

"Thank you, Snow-White."

She turned to face the bear, wracking her brain for something to say. "Are you warmer now?"

"Yes, thank you."

Rose sidled closer. "You're very polite for a bear."

"Have you met many bears, Rose-Red?"

Rose came closer still. "No, you're the first, but I've heard stories and none of the bears in the stories were polite like you."

"What were they like, Rose-Red?"

Snow moved to her sister's side, wanting to hush her. "My sister tends to be a little strange at times."

"No I'm not." Rose glared at her sister.

Snow grabbed her sister's hand and squeezed it not so gently as she tried to think of a way to change the subject. What was her sister thinking? Every story either of them had heard about bears involved them eating people. "Do you live around here?"

"In the direction of the setting sun, on the other side of the forest."

"You've been all the way to the other side of the forest?" Rose stared at him in awe, coming closer. "What is it like?"

"Much the same as the other side of the forest in the direction of the rising sun," the bear said.

"You've crossed the entire forest?" Rose asked.

The bear dipped his head. "In all directions."

"What did you see?" Rose asked.

At the same time, Snow asked, "What were you looking for?"

The bear turned his gaze on Snow and she could almost have sworn she saw sorrow in his dark eyes. When she thought he might speak to her, he turned to her sister instead.

"Many things, Rose-Red. Many things."

Rose inched closer, sitting on the floor, tucking her legs under herself. "What sort of things?"

Snow sat beside her sister and listened as the bear spoke of icy streams with fat fish, open meadows and busy villages. Ports with ships lined up at docks, merchants calling out the exotic wares they had for sale. Castles surrounded by moats and walls, mountains that towered higher than any tree and dwarves who spent winters underground and summers stealing the treasures of others.

Both girls eventually started to nod off and their mother sent them to bed. Snow curled up under her quilt, her eyes half closed as she watched the bear lying in front of the fire. As if he felt her gaze upon him, he lifted his head and looked in her direction. For a moment he stared her way, before he again put his head on his paws and settled down for the night.

The next morning, the bear was the first to wake and the sound of his claws against the wooden floorboards dragged Snow from sleep. Seeing him waiting at the door, she rose from her bed and unbolted the door to let him out.

When the bear continued to stand there, looking at her, Snow tried to think of something to say to him. "Thank you for all your stories last night."

He dipped his head in acknowledgement. "Thank you for

your hospitality." He bounded outside into the snow-covered forest.

Snow stared after him as he disappeared amongst the trees and she wondered where he planned to go next. Towards the sea? Or maybe the mountains.

"Close the door, Snow-White. You're letting the cold in," Anna called from her bed.

She slowly closed the door and crossed the room to stoke up the fire and shift the kettle into the middle to heat, her mind still full of the stories she'd heard last night. When Rose woke, she couldn't stop talking about the places the bear had spoken of until eventually Anna told her to hold her tongue.

"But they sound like such marvellous places. I really wish I could visit all of them." Rose took the bowl of reheated stew Snow handed her. "I want to be able to travel like the bear."

"Your life will be how it needs to be, Rose-Red. You complaining will not change it one bit," Anna said.

"It will be how I make it," Rose stated.

"Not until you've done your chores. Now hold your tongue and eat your meal." Anna dipped her spoon into her own bowl, after a warning look at her youngest daughter.

Once they'd finished their meal, fetched water from the well behind their home, done the morning dishes, brought in firewood and tidied the cottage, the girls bundled up to go outside and check traps. Rose continually complained about the cold and how she wished she could travel as far as the bear.

Snow eventually reached for her sister's hand. "If we had the money I'd buy us all warm clothes and you a little pony. Then you could travel miles and miles every day and see all the wonders you can imagine."

Rose grinned. "I can imagine a lot of wonders. It would take me years and years to see them all. Would you come with me? I wouldn't want to go on my own."

"Then I'd buy two ponies and we'd never be separated and we'd see everything together."

Rose's grin faded and she moved closer to her sister, slipping an arm around her waist. "I wish..." Her voice trailed off, her breath fogging the air in front of her.

By the time they'd finished

checking the traps, bringing home only one hare, and gathering more firewood, the sky was darkening. They hurried inside, both going straight to the fire to warm themselves before they prepared dinner. Their mother was already seated by the fire spinning wool.

Once again they talked Anna into another story while their meal cooked. When the scent of the hare stew filled the cottage there came a knock at the door. Both girls looked at each other.

"I'll get it." Rose dashed for the door, flinging it open. "You came back."

Snow looked across the room as the bear ambled inside. She tried to think of something to say. Something to tell him that she was glad he'd returned, but nothing sounded right when she tried the words out in her head.

Anna rose to her feet. "You're welcome to stay again, Bear. Make yourself comfortable by the fire."

"Thank you, my good woman. The night is cold and more snow is coming." The bear crossed the room and settled himself in front of the fire. This time there was no snow on his fur to make puddles on the floor.

Snow served the meal, placing a bowl in front of the bear. When they'd all eaten, Rose knelt beside the bear, begging for more stories. When he began to speak, Snow joined her sister. As she listened she noticed burrs caught in his fur and started to pull them out, throwing them in the fire. By the time he'd finished his tales the burrs were all gone. Snow rose to her feet so she could retire to bed, like her sister was doing, when the bear spoke to her.

"Thank you, Snow-White."

Not knowing what to say, she nodded and retreated to bed. Lying under her quilt she stared at the bear. Like the previous night he raised his head and watched her for a moment before he lowered it to his paws and closed his eyes.

The next few weeks passed in the same way. The bear would arrive at dinner, then after he'd eaten, tell his tales while Anna and her daughters spun wool, leaving early in the morning. Rose would endlessly talk about his tales all day while she worked with Snow then as the night came closer Rose would say over and over again that she hoped the bear would return.

When a snowstorm arrived late

one afternoon, Rose worried the bear wouldn't be able to reach them. "Last night he promised he'd tell me about ships tonight. I really, really want to go on a ship. Think how far I could travel on a ship."

"Poor Bear, I hope he does find his way here. It'll be dreadfully cold outside tonight." Snow couldn't stop sending frequent glances towards the door.

When they heard a knock on the door, both girls rushed towards it. Bear was on the doorstep, coated in snow, and didn't speak until he was in front of the fire, a puddle forming around him.

"I am sorry for the mess."

Snow fetched a cloth and shook the snow from his fur, mopping up the puddles around him. His fur remained damp and he shivered every now and then. Snow built up the fire after she'd removed the meal from it, hoping that would help warm him.

By the time their meal was over and the bear had told stories until the girls and their mother retired to bed, the bear was still shivering. Snow looked across the room at him lying as close as possible to the fire. The motherless lamb was now as far from him as it could get while still enjoying the warmth. Gathering up her quilt, Snow tiptoed across the room. The bear raised his head to look at her. She draped the quilt over him and curled up beside him, pressing her back against his slightly damp fur and tucking herself under the quilt.

"Thank you, Snow-White."

Again she was lost for words and wished she could chatter as easily as her sister. "Only my mother calls me Snow-White. Everyone else calls me Snow."

"Then I thank you, Snow. Your kindness is appreciated."

"You're welcome, Bear." She closed her eyes and listened to the sound of him breathing beside her. Eventually his shivers slowed and then stopped and his breathing deepened. Snow snuggled in closer to his warmth and fell asleep.

The bear rising in the morning woke Snow and she quietly rose to her feet and opened the door for him. "Where do you go all day, Bear?"

"Hunting."

"Game is growing scarce around here. Our traps have been empty the last two days. Where do you go hunting?"

"All through the woods. But it is

not only food I hunt. I will see you tonight, Snow, and again I thank you for your kindness."

She watched the bear disappear into the woods and quickly shut the door before the cold air woke her family. Being as quiet as possible, she returned her quilt to her bed and built up the fire to heat the food in the kettle.

By the time the food had heated, Rose and Anna were awake and joined Snow at the table to break their fast. Rose chattered about the bear's tales and complained over how boring it was in their part of the forest.

Snow finally interrupted her sister. "How can you say it's boring?"

"How can you say it isn't?"

"Bear. Every night he entertains you with his stories. Every night he tells us about all the places that we'll never get to visit except through his tales. Do you find that boring?"

Rose shook her head. "No, of course not. I just wish I could travel with him."

"I know, but at least we have his tales." Snow gathered up the bowls from the table.

"Would you come with me if I travelled to far lands?" Rose asked.

Snow smiled at her sister. "Where would you go?" She half listened as Rose spoke of the places she'd visit while they tidied the cottage then brought in more firewood and water. Next they checked their traps and found them empty, collecting firewood on their way back to the cottage, their day passing much like the ones before it.

Once again that evening, the bear

returned, but this time he brought with him a large trout and Snow threw her arms around his neck.

"Thank you, Bear. We haven't had fish in ages."

"I will pack it in snow and we will have it for dinner tomorrow night," Anna said.

Rose tugged at the bear's fur. "Come and eat so you can tell us more stories."

The bear ambled over to the fire, eating the bowl of stew they gave him before he told stories while they spun wool. When they all grew tired and clambered into their beds, Snow snuggled under her quilt and looked at the bear, alone by the fire. The lamb had finally decided it was safer to sleep near Anna, climbing onto the foot of her bed.

The bear raised his head and looked

at Snow. She met his gaze for several minutes before she smiled, gathered her quilt and crossed the room to lay down beside him, throwing the quilt over both of them.

The bear lowered his head. "Good night, Snow."

"Good night, Bear," she said softly.

They fell into a routine. Every night the bear would arrive with some game for the table. Fish, hare, birds and once even a haunch of venison. Then after the meal he would tell his tales until they retired to bed. Each night Snow joined him by the fire, covering both of them with her quilt. In the morning, while everyone else still slept Snow would let the bear out and watch as he disappeared into the forest. Some nights while she lay curled up beside him, the bear would talk softly to her so as not to wake the others. And every morning as Snow watched the bear leave, she would hope he'd return again that evening.

One morning when the weather was beginning to warm and the snow melt, she stood at the front door where the bear stood, looking silently at her.

"Is something wrong, Bear?"

"All winter the dwarves have been stuck underground and unable to wander the forest stealing and taking what isn't theirs to their caves. Now the snow is thawing I won't be back of an evening. I shall miss you and your family."

Snow threw her arms around the bear, burying her face in his fur. "When will we see you again?"

"I do not know, Snow."

Her arms remained wrapped around him. "I'll miss you."

"I have to go, Snow. You need to let go."

It took her a moment before she could draw back from him, wiping at her damp cheeks with the backs of her hands. "Will you return in the winter?"

"Maybe." He pressed his snout against her cheek before he turned away, his fur catching on the bolt.

Snow caught a glimpse of gold on the bear and she frowned, drying her eyes to see better. Before she could decide if it was a trick of the light or something else, he had disappeared into the forest, leaving behind only a few strands of hair that she gathered.

She stepped outside, closing the door behind her, taking several steps in the direction he'd taken. Her hand was pressed against her heart, but it didn't help ease the ache she felt there. Looking into the clear sky, the day barely begun, winter looked an age away. With a sigh, she turned away, going back inside to warm their morning meal.

Snow waited until Rose and Anna were seated at the table before she spoke. "Bear said he wouldn't be back while the weather is warm."

Rose stared at her sister. "What? No! Who'll tell me tales? When's he coming back?"

"He will go where he needs to go, Rose-Red. You complaining won't make him return," Anna said.

Snow's heart sank further. Even her mother didn't think Bear would return. Finishing her meal, Snow quickly tidied the cottage to the sound of her sister's grumbles, glad to finally escape outside. All day as they checked traps and gathered firewood, she couldn't stop looking for the bear. Not once did she spot him.

As the days passed, no matter how much time she spent outside, wandering further afield with her sister, she never saw him. Twice there was game left on their doorstep, but he didn't stay around to speak to her and her sadness increased.

One morning, while they ate their meal, Anna said "Today you can take the lamb back to the flock, it is old enough to survive now and the nights are much warmer. The shepherd will give you a bag of fleece for keeping it alive."

"I'm sick of spinning wool. Now Bear is no longer here it's so boring to do of an evening." Rose pushed her bowl out of the way, resting her arms and head on the table. "We never make enough to buy anything more than the ugliest of cloth."

"This winter we spun more wool then we ever have before. We should earn enough coins to buy cloth for all of us with enough left over to buy ribbons for trim," Anna said.

Rose's head jerked up. "Really?" When her mother nodded, she jumped out of her seat and stepped around the table to hug Anna. "Oh, I can't wait. Now if only we could afford a pony and I could travel miles and miles every day and see the places Bear spoke of."

Anna laughed softly. "Life will be what it needs to be, Rose-Red. Your words won't change it any."

"Maybe mine won't, but Bear's words did. I never would have spun so much wool if he hadn't kept me entertained with all his tales."

Snow couldn't feel the joy her sister felt. She would have preferred to have Bear with them than ribbons for her dress. On the walk to the shepherd, she couldn't keep from searching the forest for signs of Bear. As usual, she didn't see him.

Rose walked beside her, leading the lamb, a rope around its neck as she coaxed it forward. "If it wasn't so heavy, I'd carry it. We'll never get there before nightfall."

Rose was wrong and they reached the shepherd late morning. They delivered the lamb, collected a bag of fleece from his wife then started for home. They hadn't gone very far when they saw a large tree that had been recently felled. There was something close to the trunk jumping around in the long grass.

Snow grabbed her sister's arm when she would have gone forward. "We don't know what it is."

"We didn't know anything about Bear either and look how marvellous that turned out."

Snow nodded, letting her sister's arm go. "Be careful though." She took her sister's hand, slowly moving forward, stopping when she saw it was a dwarf. His lined and weathered face was screwed up in anger. His pure white beard, nearly longer than his height of three feet, was caught in a crevice of the tree. He jumped about, his hands wrapped around the middle of his beard, as he tugged and pulled at it.

Noticing the girls, he turned his fiery red eyes on them. "Help me you stupid girls. What are you doing standing there watching? Can't you see I'm caught?"

"What were you doing?" Rose asked.

"Stupid girl. Can't you see I was trying to break up the tree for firewood? Look. Over there." He pointed towards some long grass. "There's the wedge I had driven in, but it sprang out and the tree caught my beard. Hurry up you odious creatures and help me."

The girls dropped the bag of fleece and stepped forward, trying to pull the beard from the crevice. Having no luck, they used the wedge to lever the crevice apart, but still the beard was caught.

Rose stared at the tree, hands on her hips. "Maybe we should go back and ask the shepherd to help. This is impossible."

"Senseless. The pair of you are senseless. Why would I want you to fetch someone else? There are already too many of you odious creatures here," the dwarf snarled.

"He's not very nice," Rose said. "It'd serve him right if we left him here."

Snow patted her pockets and found a pair of scissors she'd picked up earlier that morning when they'd tidied the cottage. "I can help you." She withdrew the scissors and cut off the end of the dwarf's beard.

The dwarf ranted at the girls for ruining his beard. They stepped back at his shouts.

"You still have nearly two feet left," Snow said, quickly wishing she hadn't when his shouting worsened.

He finished with, "Bad luck to you," then grabbed a bag that had been lying amongst the roots of the tree and ran away.

Rose pointed after the dwarf. "There was gold in that bag. I saw it. Beastly creature. He could have at least given us a coin for helping him."

About to answer, Snow caught a glimpse of something running through the forest, in the direction of the dwarf. Something dark. For a moment she thought it might be Bear. It was foolishness. Not once had she seen him since the snow had thawed. Why would she see him now? Sighing, she returned the scissors to her pocket and picked up the bag of fleece. "Let's go home, Rose."

Rose walked beside her sister. "Do you ever wonder where Bear is?"

All the time, Snow started to say, but changed her mind. "Yes."

"Do you think he's fine? Do you think he'll come back and tell us more stories?"

She thought of the glimpse she'd caught of something moving through the forest. "I hope so."

The rest of the week was uneventful and every morning Rose asked if today they could take the wool to market. Each time Anna would tell her they should spin a little more first and sent them out to do their chores. Now spring had well and truly arrived, the girls prepared the vegetable patch for seeds and planted them. After a week of working in the garden they were so sick of it, when Anna asked them one morning to catch fish for their dinner, they were glad to take a break.

Rose chattered away as they walked to the brook. Her words ended abruptly, when ahead they saw something jumping around at the water's edge. "What is that?"

"I don't know." Snow took a couple of cautious steps forward. "It can't be." She strode forward until she could clearly see the creature. "It is."

"What awful luck. I wonder what the dwarf's trying to do."

"Maybe he's planning to play in the water, but if he jumps around like that in the water he'll scare away all the fish for miles around," Snow said.

"Come on, then. I want fish for dinner. He can go and play somewhere else." Rose marched towards the brook, stopping on the bank. "What are you doing? You're not planning to go in the water are you?"

"I'm not such a fool as you pair. Look! Look!" The dwarf pointed in the water. "Can't you see that fish trying to pull me in by my beard?"

"Look out!" Snow jumped forward and grabbed the dwarf's arm before the fish had the chance to pull him into the water.

Rose grabbed his other arm and together they tried to drag him away from the water's edge. "It's no good." Her face was going red from the effort. "That fish isn't about to let go."

"I brought my scissors with me in case our lines got tangled," Snow said.

"Don't you dare cut my beard," the dwarf shouted.

"Do something, Snow. I can't hold him a minute longer," Rose said.

Snow let go of the dwarf to pull out her scissors, cutting more from the end of his beard, as he screamed at her. She moved away from him the moment he was free, still holding onto her scissors as she warily watched him, his beard half the length it had been.

The dwarf grasped the end of his beard. "I'm disfigured. I won't be able to show my face to my people without being ridiculed. You uncivil beasts." He grabbed a sack from amongst the reeds. "I wish you had been made to run the soles off your shoes and have to forever walk around barefoot!" he cursed and with a last glare for each of them, he slung the sack over his shoulder before he ran off into the forest.

"Ungrateful wretch. Did you see what he had, Snow?"

Snow shook her head, returning her scissors to her pocket.

"He had pearls this time. There

were pearls in that sack. Come help me look. Maybe he dropped one." Rose searched among the reeds, but found nothing.

Snow tossed her line into the brook and watched as her sister searched and muttered. A sound drew her attention and she caught a glimpse of something large and dark moving quickly through the forest in the direction of the dwarf. She sighed. If only she could see Bear and not just shadows that made her think of him.

Rose came and sat beside Snow, throwing her own line in the water. "So unfair. He could have given us a pearl for helping him. That's twice now we've helped him. Ungrateful beast."

"Never mind, Rose. Soon we'll go to the markets and earn our own coins to spend."

That night, after a meal of fish, Snow lay awake in her bed, staring at the banked fire where she and Bear had once slept. Missing him, she gathered up her quilt and wrapped it around herself before she lay down in front of the glowing coals. It didn't help and she continued to lay awake for hours before exhaustion dragged her into sleep only to wake early in the morning to stare at the embers of the fire.

Unable to stay inside a moment longer, she returned her quilt to her bed and quietly slipped outside. On the doorstep was a hare. Snow ran forward, looking around for Bear, but he was already gone.

"Where are you?" she asked softly, staring into the dense forest. "Where are you?" With a sigh, she gathered the hare and returned inside to warm the morning meal.

It was nearly a week before Anna finally told her daughters it was time to take the wool to market. Rose shrieked excitedly, throwing her arms around her mother.

Anna looked at Snow over Rose's shoulder. "Make sure you get a good price for the wool and buy enough cloth to make new dresses for each of us."

Snow nodded before she gathered up the wool and packed some fruit and cheese to eat on their journey. Rose bundled up their quilts as it would take them more than a day to reach the market.

When they set out to the market, Anna stood at the door, waving to them. "Buy some needles and thread as well and take care. Make sure you look out for each other."

Rose walked backwards, waving to their mother, a grin on her face. "See you tomorrow afternoon." Stumbling on a rock, she faced forward. "I wish we could keep on going and didn't have to come back for ages and ages. Wouldn't you love to explore new places?"

Once she would have immediately said no. Now Snow wasn't so sure. Their cottage seemed a lonely bleak place these days. "I don't know, Rose."

Hitching the bundle on her back first, Rose reached out and clasped Snow's hand. "Is something wrong? You seem to get quieter each day."

Snow met her sister's gaze, seeing that her eyes were clouded with worry. She lightly squeezed her hand.

"I'm well. I'm just trying to decide what colour ribbon I should get to trim my dress."

"Are you sure?"

"It's been years and years since we've been able to afford ribbons, aren't you having trouble deciding which colour?"

Rose's eyes cleared and she grinned. "I was thinking I might get several shorter lengths and trim my dress with different colours. It'll be like wearing a rainbow. If we're going to be stuck with the same drab, serviceable cloth it's going to need something dramatic to cheer it up."

Snow nodded and smiled, letting her sister's chatter wash over her, as her gaze searched the forest they walked through. After some time, even Rose's words came to an end and they walked in silence.

Eventually they reached the road, which started as a narrow dirt track and met up with a wider one. The road had two deep ruts from the many carts that had travelled along it over the years, but currently was empty and the two girls travelled it alone.

When the sun began to set, Snow looked for a place they could spend the night. She found a sheltered spot, off the road, where they laid their bundles down and gathered firewood to make a small fire. They'd need it to keep warm when it cooled off in the night. After they'd eaten, the girls rolled up in their quilts and lay beside each other near the fire. Snow was on the side away from the fire, having given her sister the coveted warmest spot.

She lay awake, listening to the

night sounds, propping her head up on her hand to watch the flames dance and crackle. A howl sounded in the darkness, followed by a growl. She tried to see what was out there, but it was impossible to see in the dark.

"Snow?"

"Yes?"

"What was that?"

"I don't know. It's gone now. Go to sleep, Rose."

When the night remained quiet, Snow followed her own advice and finally fell asleep. As she slept, she dreamt she was once again sleeping beside Bear. His warm body pressed against her, feeling his fur beneath her hand when she reached for him. At her back her sister breathed softly, nowhere near as warm as the bear she snuggled up to.

Early morning light woke Snow from a deep sleep and before she opened her eyes, she reached for Bear, her hand encountering only grass. Disappointment hit her and she opened her eyes. It had only been a dream. The ache in her heart increased as she made herself shake her sister awake so they could continue to the market.

When they were on the road, Snow forced a smile to her lips as her sister almost danced beside her, chatting away nearly non-stop. They hadn't travelled far when the road took them out of the forest and across a heath.

"Look." Rose pointed to the sky.

Snow looked up to see a large bird hovering in the air, flying round and round above them. The bird swooped down and Snow raced forward to see what it was trying to grab. "It's the dwarf. We have to save him."

Rose ran beside her sister. "He wouldn't save us."

"The bird will carry him off."

"And good riddance to him too," Rose said.

"Rose!"

"Oh very well. I'll help the ungrateful beast."

Dropping their bundles, the girls continued to run forward until they could grab the dwarf's legs as the bird struggled to gain height. He screamed and shrieked at both them and the bird. Finally they managed to pull him from the claws of the bird and he tumbled to the ground.

Jumping indignantly to his feet, the dwarf glared at them with his fiery red eyes. "You tore my coat. Look at it. It's full of holes and completely ruined. Useless creatures."

"At least we didn't have to cut your beard this time," Rose pointed out.

Her words brought another tirade and Snow rolled her eyes, wishing her sister hadn't bothered mentioning the beard. She walked away, grabbing her bundle and ignoring the dwarf who still yelled at them.

"I told you he'd be ungrateful." Rose stopped beside Snow, hoisting her own bundle onto her back.

"At least we did the right thing," Snow said.

Rose eyed the dwarf who still yelled at them, following them as they headed back to the road. "I don't know about that. I'm sure someone would have thanked us if we'd let the bird cart him away."

With one last insult, the dwarf

grabbed a sack that had been hidden in a pile of rocks near the road and hurried away towards the forest.

Rose pointed after him. "Look at that. A sack of precious stones and he didn't even offer us one for saving his life. All he did was complain about his miserable old coat."

Snow took hold of her sister's hand. "Never mind, Rose. You should be used to him by now."

"It still isn't right. Greedy dwarf. He could have given us something. A coin, a pearl, a precious stone. Anything." Rose momentarily fell silent as they continued towards the market that was held in their closest town. "Doesn't it make you angry? Don't you think he should have given us something for saving his life?"

Snow met her sister's gaze, not feeling any of the anger she could see filling her eyes. How would precious stones bring Bear back? They wouldn't. Words her mother would have spoken came to her mind. "The dwarf will do what he wants. You being angry won't change him."

Rose reached for her sister, sliding an arm around her waist. "Don't say that, Snow. You sound as sad as our mother."

She forced a smile to her lips. "Then stop worrying about that ungrateful dwarf."

"He's all forgotten."

Snow nodded, unable to think of anything else to say. It took all her effort to keep the smile in place. But she didn't have to worry, her sister started to talk about all the things she hoped to see when they reached the market.

They arrived late morning and

Snow was able to get a good price for the wool and purchase the items their mother had sent them to buy. Choosing ribbons took far longer as Rose couldn't decide which few to buy when there were so many choices. In the end Snow said she'd choose so they wouldn't be late home and Rose grudgingly made her choices.

Setting out for home, after they'd eaten their midday meal, the girls had nearly reached the forest when they saw the dwarf.

Rose clutched at her sister's arm and pointed towards the dwarf. "Snow!" Rose spoke her sister's name in a hushed whisper.

Snow was unable to speak at all. The dwarf sat on a rock, his back to them as he polished precious stones that were spread out on the sack they'd been in earlier. They sparkled and glittered in the rays of the afternoon sun, as many colours as there had been in the ribbons in the market. Taking another step forward, a stick snapped under her foot.

The dwarf jumped up, turning to face them. "You." He pointed an accusing finger at them. "Why are you standing there staring? Go away vile creatures." He started to gather up the stones, returning them to the sack, all the time cursing their presence.

"I don't know why we ever bothered to save him," Rose muttered.

Snow began to walk forward again. "I'm beginning to wonder too."

A growl came from the forest and all three of them froze, facing the sound. A bear burst from among the trees, wild eyed and snarling, leaping at the dwarf.

"No, Mr Bear. Please no. Spare me. Take those vile creatures instead." The dwarf dodged to the side, gesturing toward the girls.

Snow clung to Rose, not knowing what to do. Should they run and risk catching the bear's attention and have him chasing them or stay and hope he'd be satisfied with the dwarf.

The bear attacked the dwarf again, snarling. Sharp teeth were visible and the wild look remained in his eyes.

Once more the dwarf managed to avoid the paw that struck out at him. "Please, Mr Bear. I would be tough and barely a mouthful. Take those wicked girls instead. Vicious creatures that they are. They cut off my beard and tore up my coat. Take them instead."

The bear snarled, attacking again. This time his large paw connected with the dwarf, who was flung to the side, his words cut off in a scream that ended abruptly.

Rose screamed and turned to run, her hand grasping Snow's as she tugged her along with her. "Run, Snow. Hurry."

Snow looked behind, stumbling. The bear stared after them, no longer snarling, the wild look gone from his eyes. Surely it couldn't be their bear.

"Snow."

The bear called after her and she tugged her hand from her sister's grasp, stopping to face him. "Bear?" Her voice was hesitant as she took a step towards him.

"Snow!" The bear loped towards

her, his fur falling away as he rose on two legs, becoming a man dressed in fine clothes. He threw his arms around her, drawing her close. "Snow."

She reached up to tentatively touch his cheek, the skin smooth and warm. "How can this be?" Her bear was a man? Impossible. He couldn't be.

He smiled. "I'm Calum, the son of a king, and that dwarf bewitched me and stole the treasures of my family. I have had to run around the forest trying to find our treasures and kill the dwarf so I could break the spell."

Rose reached their side. "No wonder you had all those stories to tell. As a prince you must have seen so many marvellous sights."

Keeping one arm around Snow, the prince held out a hand to Rose who took hold of it. "And so shall you Rose." He turned to Snow. "So will both of you. But first I have to find the dwarf's cave and my family's treasures."

Snow could barely take in all that was happening. Her sister almost bounced on the spot, a grin on her face, and Calum kept his arm around her waist. She wanted her bear back, the bear she'd grown to love.

"There's a sack of precious stones over there." Rose pointed to the sack that had spilled part of its contents in the grass.

"There are more than just those. There is gold, pearls, jewels and numerous other treasures." He turned to Snow. "You've barely spoken a word. Tell me you're glad to see me."

She could only stare at him, nodding. Her hand reached out and touched his gold brocade vest and she remembered the last day she'd seen him leave their cottage and the glimpse of gold when he'd caught himself on the bolt. Her attention was momentarily caught by her sister hurrying over to gather up the precious stones in the grass.

"Snow?" His smile faded. "Are you glad to see me?"

"Yes." But she would miss her bear. A comfortable creature who didn't make her feel tongue tied like the finely dressed gentleman standing in front of her. How was she meant to talk to a prince?

Calum stared intently at her for a moment. "I have to find the dwarf's cave."

"I'm coming too." Rose rejoined them, carrying the sack of precious stones. "And you better not be like the dwarf. I want a reward for helping."

Calum chuckled. "A reward you will have, but first we have to find the cave." He turned to Snow. "What about you? Are you joining us in our search?"

Snow nodded, staring at Calum. Was there any of her bear left in him? Or was he a complete stranger?

"Of course she is," Rose said. "An adventure is exactly what she needs." She grabbed her sister's hand and tugged her away from the prince. "We'll search over here."

Snow let her sister take her to a scattering of rocks and boulders. She looked back at the prince, who stood in the same place, staring after her. She froze. His eyes. They were the eyes of her bear.

"What is wrong with you?" Rose hissed.

Snow turned to her sister. "What do you mean?"

Rose tugged her further away from Calum. "Don't give me that rubbish. I thought you liked our bear and now you're treating him like some stranger."

"He's a prince. What interest can he have in us? Think of all his tales. All the interesting people he spoke about. He probably knows all of them. Who are we? Two girls who've lived their entire lives in a little cottage in the middle of a forest. When he was a bear and it was the middle of winter, he needed us. Now he's a prince again."

Rose wrapped her arms around her. "Oh Snow, he won't treat us different, I'm sure of it."

But Snow didn't feel anywhere near as certain as her sister did. Once he'd found his treasure, he'd return home and they'd never see him again. Not even in winter. For a few seconds she was tempted to beg him not to look for the treasure. Beg him to stay with them, but he had a family waiting. They deserved to know he was human again. She pulled away from her sister. "Come on, let's find that treasure so you can get your reward." Her gaze scanned the area, looking for any cave entrances.

"I want a pony. No, make that two ponies so we can travel together and explore marvellous places."

It was Snow who found the entrance, hidden behind a boulder, that wasn't pushed properly into place. She stared at the darkness behind the boulder for a moment before she called Rose and Calum.

The prince pushed at the boulder until they could squeeze through. Inside, sitting next to the tunnel wall, was a lantern that Snow lit and held up so they could see the tunnel leading downwards.

"If you don't wish to go down there with me you're welcome to wait here," Calum said.

Snow stared at him. His deep voice still sounded very much like her bear, just not as gruff. She continued to stare at him, memorising his face. It wouldn't be long now and she'd never see him again. He was her bear and she wanted to spend every moment possible with him. "We'll go with you."

The prince smiled, reaching for the

lantern, his other hand taking hers. "I'm glad."

They walked side by side in the narrow tunnel, Rose following closely behind them. The tunnel was silent save for their footsteps echoing around them. Snow almost wished the tunnel would never end. That she could walk beside Calum forever, holding his hand. The tunnel opened into a cavern and the lantern sent patterns of light over the walls as it landed on jewels, gems and coins that reflected the light.

Rose rushed forward, lifting up a tiara and placing it on her head with a grin. "Do you think it suits me?"

The prince laughed. "Of course, dear Rose. Somewhere in amongst all this there should be a matching necklace that goes with it."

"Really? I need to find it." Rose

looked through sacks and piles of random items.

Letting go of Snow's hand, the prince stepped forward, putting the lantern on the floor as he reached for one of the larger sacks. "My sword should be around here somewhere."

Snow watched the two of them, storing up memories for a future without her bear. They chatted to each other, smiles on their faces. Rose held up necklaces and bracelets, asking about who owned them and where they'd been worn. Calum's voice filled the cavern as he told the tale of each piece. She closed her eyes, listening to the stories, the sound so familiar. He was definitely her bear. Opening her eyes she stared at the prince. She'd seen him change before her eyes and she recognised his voice. There could be no mistake. Her bear was a prince who'd soon return to his castle and probably never think of her again.

It was no use postponing the inevitable. She'd help him find his sword so he could return to his world and she could return to mourning the loss of her bear. Snow was nearly at the far side of the cavern when the prince shouted triumphantly.

"I've found it." He held the sword aloft, a grin on his face.

Snow started to walk back towards him, Rose already at his side.

The grin disappeared from Calum's face. "Snow! Run!" He ran towards her, brandishing his sword.

At the sound of a snarl coming from behind her, Snow glanced over her shoulder just as a vicious beast leapt at her. She flung herself to the side, falling among bags of gold coins that spilled their contents around her. Struggling to get up, she saw the beast come for her again.

Calum jumped between her and the beast, attacking with his sword. The beast snarled and snapped, trying to get past the blade that Calum eventually stabbed deep into its body. Then he was kneeling beside her, pressing her to him. "Snow. Tell me you're unhurt. Snow, please talk to me."

Rose reached her side, crouching next to her. "Snow?" Her voice was filled with concern.

"I'm fine." Her words were muffled against Calum's chest. She wrapped her arms around him, holding him as tight as he held her, trembling from her brush with death. "I dreamt of you last night."

He pulled back slightly to stare

down at her, a smile forming. "I chased a pack of wolves away and waited until you slept to move in close. I knew I should have been searching for the dwarf, but I couldn't stay away."

"You were there? It wasn't a dream?"

"I was there." His hand cupped her face. "I wanted to wake you and talk to you, but I couldn't."

"Why not?"

"Because I wouldn't have been able to bring myself to leave your side the next day." He gestured around them. "The dwarf has beggared my family. I had to find their treasure. It was more important than me killing the dwarf to break the spell he'd cast on me."

"How will you get all this back to your home?"

"I'll take some of the gold coins

and go to the nearest village and buy horses and carts."

"We'll protect it for you while you're gone," Rose said.

The prince reached out to ruffle her hair. "Then I shan't be worried about it. I'll know it's in good hands." He stood, drawing Snow up with him, his gaze still on Rose. "If you can put everything back into the sacks it'll make it easier to load the carts when I return."

With a nod, Rose began her task.

Calum drew Snow to the tunnel opening. "I'm almost afraid to let you out of my sight. Be careful while I'm gone. There are no other beasts in here, but others might find the tunnel."

She stared up at him, holding back the words 'don't go' that continued to echo in her mind. "I'll be here, waiting for you." She didn't know how she'd ever let him go once he was ready to take his treasure home.

He drew Snow close, his lips meeting hers. Minutes passed before he finally drew away. "I'll leave the lantern with you." He turned and hurried along the tunnel towards the entrance of the cave.

Snow watched him until he was no longer visible, her fingers pressed against her lips. It was several minutes before she turned away to stare at the treasures that needed to be put into the numerous partly filled sacks. At least it would give her something to focus on while she waited for Calum to return. Anything was better than thinking about what it was going to be like when he left and she never saw him again.

When he did return, he brought

several large men with him, all of them carrying lanterns. They soon had the carts filled with treasure and had gathered their bundles they'd left forgotten near the road in all the excitement. Snow sat beside the prince on one of the carts while Rose sat next to the man on the cart behind them. They travelled much quicker through the forest and Snow nodded off as they travelled through the night, her head resting on Calum's shoulder. She fought to stay awake, wanting to cherish every moment, but tiredness swamped her.

When she woke, it was early morning, and Calum's arm was around her waist keeping her close. She dreaded the moment when he would say goodbye and she never saw him again. Her gaze was drawn to his face. There was still a little time yet before she reached that point.

They arrived at the cottage mid morning and Anna came out to meet them. Rose dragged her from cart to cart, showing her the treasures they'd rescued. Calum helped Snow down from the cart, leading her inside to stand in front of the fireplace.

"I couldn't believe it the first time you slept here beside me. I couldn't imagine why you'd even care what happened to a wild creature like I was. And then every night you slept next to me, sharing your only quilt. Walking away from here was the hardest thing I've ever done, but what could I have offered you? I was a bear."

Snow smiled. "That would have been enough."

"Not for me. You deserved more

than a wild creature. You can't imagine how relieved I am to be human again." He knelt on one knee, taking her hand. "Snow, will you do me the honour of becoming my bride."

Snow stared down at him, barely able to believe what she'd heard. Hope rose and she pressed a hand to her mouth, a smile starting to form.

Rose squealed from the doorway. "Say yes, Snow. Say yes."

Ignoring her sister, Snow continued to stare at Calum, trying to find the words she wanted to speak.

Calum turned to Rose. "Go away, Rose."

"But I need to know what she says. Hurry up, Snow."

"If you leave right now and close the door behind you, I'll give you that tiara you're so fond of."

With another squeal, Rose slammed the door shut and screamed for her mother, her excited words blending together into nonsense.

"Snow?" His eyes filled with worry. "Say something, Snow."

She finally found her voice, dropping her hand from her mouth, looking into the familiar eyes. "Yes."

He stood, crushing her to him. "You had me worried for a minute. I thought you were going to say no."

"I would have said yes, even if you were still a bear."

"I can't wait to introduce you to my family. They'll love you."

Before Snow had a chance to worry about meeting the king, Calum's lips met hers. She slid her arms around his neck, holding onto him tightly.

Anna came inside, clearing her throat.

With one last quick kiss, Calum turned to his soon to be mother-in-law. "I've asked your daughter to be my bride and she has accepted. I know she'll want you and her sister with her when I take her to my family's castle. There's plenty of space for everyone and my family would make you welcome."

Rose squealed again, rushing inside to throw her arms around both Calum and Snow. "I really want to live in a castle. It'll be marvellous. When can we leave? Now?"

Anna shook her head. "Once I have packed my things and dug up your rose bushes."

"I'll help." Rose rushed around, gathering things she thought her mother might want to keep.

Calum chuckled. "She reminds me a little of my younger brother. He lives for adventure."

Rose paused in her mad rush. "Really? How old is he?"

"Only two years your senior. He's been trying to convince our father to let him go away to sea."

"A ship? That'd be better than a castle. I want to go too. What about you, Snow? Don't you want to go on a ship?"

Snow shook her head, sliding her arm around Calum's waist. "No. I'm sure I'll find more than enough adventure, living in a castle, without needing to go away to sea." She watched as her mother packed the large book into the chest at the foot of her bed, on top of the three quilts. Thinking of the first night of snow last winter when her sister had opened the door to find a bear on their doorstep, she couldn't help smiling.

"What are you thinking of," Calum asked.

She looked up at him, her smile still in place. "My bear."

The Frog Prince

Escaping insincere condolences, Calandra wanders far from home and comes across a spring. Losing her golden ball in the spring she fears it's lost forever. A frog fetches it for her in exchange for a promise she's forced to keep.

*

People have been telling stories since the beginning of time. Fairytales, folklore, myths and legends are among some of the stories that have been told over and over through the centuries. The basic story remains the same, but each storyteller adds their own style, sometimes adding something unique to the tale.

*

This story was written by an Australian author using Australian spelling.

The Frog Prince

Calandra decided that if she had to thank one more person she was likely to throw something at them. Not one single person here cared that Queen Nicoline had passed away four years ago. All they cared was that her father, King Kobus, had declared it a national day of mourning and most saw it as a holiday. She needed to escape their insincerity.

Slipping through the crowd, she headed for her bedroom. Once there she changed into something more appropriate for a walk through the woods and grabbed her bonnet. It might be evening, but at this time of year the sun didn't set until late. She'd be alone out there and not have to force herself to smile and say thank you to an endless crowd of people.

She started to turn towards the door when the golden ball, she'd dropped on her bed that morning, caught her attention. Hesitant steps brought her to the edge of the bed and she picked up the ball, holding it against her chest. Her eyes closed as she remembered her mother playing ball games with her. The image wasn't clear and try as she might she couldn't bring her mother's face to mind. She'd been nearly thirteen when her mother had passed away. Surely that was old enough to remember exactly what her mother had looked like.

Her father often told her she reminded him of her mother with her golden curls and green eyes, but she'd much rather be able to recall what Nicoline had looked like. Still holding the golden ball she left her room before someone came looking for her.

It was quiet in the woods with no one telling her how terribly her mother was missed and what a sad day it had been when she'd passed away. She'd be surprised if more than a handful had actually meant what they'd said. She played with the ball as she walked, turning it in her hands and sometimes tossing it into the air. Why couldn't she clearly picture her mother anymore? When she returned to the castle later she'd have to study the portrait that had been painted a couple of years before her mother had passed away. Look at it until the image was firmly fixed in her mind so she could never forget what her mother had looked like.

Lost in thought Calandra walked much further than she'd planned, coming across a spring she'd never seen before. Deciding to have a rest before she returned, she sat beside the spring. She continued to toss the golden ball in her hands, catching it each time. Once she'd played a similar game with her mother. It seemed so long ago now. Again she threw the ball up and this time when she tried to catch it, the ball slipped from her hands and bounced across the ground and into the spring.

She jumped to her feet, crying out in dismay. She couldn't stand to lose the ball too. Peering into the water she saw the ball far down at the bottom, barely visible. Kneeling at the edge of the spring, she rolled back her sleeve and tried to reach the ball. It was impossible. The spring was too deep. Something brushed against her arm and she pulled back, shrieking as she sat down hard on the ground. Tears came to her eyes. The ball was lost to her. Like her mother.

"I'd give all my fine clothes and jewels to have it back. Why did I bring it with me today?" She wiped at her tears with her dry hand.

A large frog stuck his head up out the water. "Why are you crying?"

Calandra shrieked again, scrambling back even further from the edge of the spring. Was that the slimy creature that had brushed against her arm while she had been trying to reach for the ball? She shuddered to think it might have been.

"Is there anything I can do to help you?"

"How can you help?" She rose to her feet, taking another step back from the spring. "I lost my ball in your spring. How can you expect to get it out for me?" He was just like all those annoying people who'd been telling her all day how much her mother was missed. And she'd had enough of them. "I shouldn't be talking to you. You're a nasty, disgusting little frog and I'm a princess. How dare you even talk to me." The words didn't make her feel any better. They actually made her feel worse.

"I want none of your fine clothes or jewels if I fetch the ball for you.

All I ask is that you let me live with you, eat from your golden plate, sleep upon your bed beside you and that you love me."

Calandra laughed. "Is that all?" Who did he think he was? "Sure, you can have all that. As long as you fetch my ball for me." Nasty little creature that he should mock her that way. How dare he be so cruel?

"Your word that you agree to my terms."

She waved airily. "Yes, of course." The day had been terrible right from the start. Maybe on the next anniversary of her mother's death she'd remain in bed until it was over. She would refuse to listen when her father said it was her duty to accept the condolences of the people. Why should she have to listen to the empty words of people who didn't care?

The frog ducked beneath the water and Calandra was about to start for home when the frog popped up again. He held her golden ball in his mouth. After moving closer to the edge of the spring, he spat the ball on the ground.

Calandra dashed forward and grabbed it. "My ball." Moving away from the edge of the spring, she stared at it in amazement. She'd thought for sure it was lost. As lost to her as her mother was.

"Help me out of the spring and take me home with you."

Her gaze was drawn from the ball to the frog that was still in the spring. "You must be joking." Surely he hadn't been serious. "You want to sleep on my bed?" There'd been other demands, but she couldn't remember them. That one had been bad enough. She backed away, slowly shaking her head. There was no way she was going to let that slimy creature sleep on her bed. It'd probably give her nightmares.

"Wait, Princess. Don't leave without me."

She shuddered at the thought of him sleeping beside her. Turning away she raced back the way she'd come, clutching the damp ball to her chest. When she arrived at the castle it was to find that most of the guests had departed. Finally something was going right in her otherwise miserable day. Avoiding the few people that were still about, she hurried to her bedroom, deciding the best thing she could do was go to sleep early and hope that tomorrow was a far better day.

Her sleep wasn't as restful as she'd

hoped and she tossed and turned, dreaming the frog was calling out for her to wait. She ran and he followed, making an unnerving noise as he jumped behind her. A wet kind of plopping sound that she couldn't escape.

Giving up on sleep she rose early and, after she'd dressed, she sought out her mother's portrait. She stared at the painting, wondering why she couldn't remember her mother this clearly. Especially her gentle smile and the kind look in her green eyes.

"You remind me so much of her."

Calandra turned to see her father stood nearby. Did he find it hard to remember what Nicoline looked like too? She couldn't bring herself to ask. "I'm nowhere near as beautiful as Mother was."

Kobus closed the distance between

them and put an arm around her shoulders as he stood looking up at the portrait. "You grow more like her every day."

She didn't know how to reply so thought it best to remain silent rather than argue his comment.

"Have you broken your fast yet?"

"No." She'd come here first. Had needed to remind herself what Nicoline had looked like.

"Neither have I. Come join me for something to eat before I take a morning ride."

The rest of the day passed uneventfully and Calandra left her golden ball, which she often carried around with her, in her room. She didn't want to risk losing it again. By dinner, she'd almost completely forgotten about yesterday's misadventure.

Sitting at the table, she heard a strange noise floating in the window. It sounded like something coming up the marble staircase to the front door. A strange sound that reminded her of something she couldn't quite place.

"Princess? Open the door, Princess." She heard someone knocking.

Curiosity had her hurrying to the front door and opening it, wondering where the footman was that normally answered the door. She looked outside and saw no one there.

"Princess, I've had a long journey to reach your side. Please pick me up and carry me to the table so I might dine with you."

Calandra looked down and shrieked to see the frog sitting on the doorstep. She slammed the door and raced back to the dining room to find her father now seated there.

"Is something wrong?"

She nodded then quickly shook her head.

"Is that a yes or a no?"

She sat at the table. "It was only a nasty frog at the front door. I was surprised to see him again."

"Where did you see him the first time?"

"I went for a walk yesterday evening and my ball fell into a spring. The frog rescued it for me."

"Then why is he here?"

"I think he wants to live with us. I may have kind of agreed that he could. But I didn't think he'd be able to get out of the spring."

"Go and let him in." The king's voice was firm.

"But, Father-"

"A princess should always keep her word. Now go and let him in."

She reluctantly rose from the table. "You don't understand. He wants to sleep on my bed."

"Then you shouldn't have given him your word that he could. Go and let him in."

Seeing her father wasn't about to relent, Calandra walked to the front door and swung it open. She stared down at the frog that was still on the doorstep.

"Will you pick me up, Princess, and carry me to the dining room so I may eat with you?"

"No, but you may come inside." She held the door open further and stepped out of the way, cringing at the sound he made as he jumped across the floor. It was the sound she'd heard in her dreams. As soon as he was inside she closed the door and headed back to the dining room. Behind her she could hear him following. How was she to convince her father that she couldn't eat while a frog dined at the table with them?

She reached the table before the frog and sat down, staring at her food. This day wasn't turning out to be much better than the previous one. When the frog came to a stop beside her chair, she looked down at him. His green skin looked slimy and damp and his eyes protruded from his head, looking unnaturally big compared to the rest to him.

"Pick me up and set me on the chair beside you, Princess."

She first looked to her father, but saw there'd be no help there. Reaching out, she gingerly picked the frog up, trying desperately not to drop him. She doubted the frog or her father would be impressed if she did. Once he was on the seat beside her she wanted to run from the room and wash her hands. She made do with wiping them on her napkin.

"Can you move your plate closer to me, Princess? I can't dine from your golden plate when it's that far from me."

Another glance towards her father showed that he waited for her to comply. Clamping her teeth together, she held back the protests she wanted to make. There was no way she was having another piece of food from that plate. She slid it close and watched as the frog helped himself to her food. Her stomach churned and she looked away. How long would he expect to be able to stay with her?

"I haven't had a meal this wonderful in years," the frog said.

"I'm surprised you've ever had a meal like this," Calandra said.

"Calandra." There was a warning note in her father's tone. "Why not ask your guest if he'd like more to eat?"

She'd rather ask her guest when he was leaving. How could her father do this to her? It was a frog. Surely he didn't expect her to let him stay as long as he wanted. She turned to the frog. "Would you like more to eat?" It was an effort to keep her tone civil.

"No, I'm quite full thank you. What I would like is to retire for the evening. Will you carry me to your chamber and put me on your bed so I can go to sleep?"

Once more she turned to her

father, hoping he'd tell her it wasn't necessary.

"See to your guest, Calandra."

She stared at him. "You want me to let him sleep on my bed beside me."

"Did you promise him he could?"

Telling her father that she couldn't remember all her promise probably wasn't a good idea. "I might have."

Kobus turned to the frog. "What exactly were the terms of your agreement?"

"The princess agreed to let me live with her, eat from her golden plate, sleep upon the bed beside her and to love me."

"You can't make me do all that." The words exploded from her. No way could he make her love him. Surely he didn't really expect that of her.

The king rose from his seat. "If you

gave your word then you're obliged to give him exactly what you promised."

"But…" Her father couldn't expect her to love such a slimy creature. How could the frog have expected it? She'd been wrong. This day was turning out worse than yesterday.

"It's time to retire for the night. I suggest you make your guest comfortable." Kobus strode from the room.

Calandra stared after her father, wanting to call him back and beg him to tell her the frog didn't have to share her bed. How was she meant to sleep with such a creature beside her?

"Princess, I am quite tired after such a long journey."

Calandra glared at the frog, rising from her seat to pick him up. She held him out from her, trying not to think about how his slimy skin felt against her hands. It wasn't fair that her father should expect this of her. Reaching her room, she set the frog on the very edge of her bed. Her lips thinned when he jumped over to sit on one half of her pillow.

"Have I left enough space for you, Princess?"

Her hands curled into fists. She wanted to tell him to leave her alone and then throw him out the window. Somehow she managed to answer him. "There's plenty of space for me." If she could bring herself to lie down beside him. "I might read for awhile before I go to sleep." She gestured towards the comfortable chair in a corner of her room.

"That would be lovely. It's been a long time since I've heard a story. Set me on the arm of the chair and you can read to me until you're ready to retire."

She shook her head. "I never agreed to that."

"But you did agree to let me sleep beside you."

She wanted to scream in frustration. "Why couldn't you have accepted the fine clothes and jewels I offered?"

"They are of no use to me."

Calandra sighed heavily. "Fine." She walked around to the other side of the bed and dropped onto it. "Go to sleep."

"Aren't you going to put the light out?"

"No." There was no way she was going to sleep beside the creature in the dark. It was bad enough that she had to share the bed with him without plunging the room into darkness as well.

"How are we meant to sleep with the light on?"

"I thought you were tired."

"I am, but the light will make it impossible to sleep."

A scream threatened to escape as she glared at the frog. "If I turn the light out, will you stay on that side of the pillow?"

"Yes."

The satisfied tone of voice the frog used made her want to push him off the bed. Instead, she rose to her feet and brought the lamp back to the bed with her, not putting it out until she was sitting on the edge of the bed. "Are you still in the same place?"

"Yes, Princess."

Setting the dark lamp on the floor, she lay on the edge of the bed. And as hard as she tried, she couldn't sleep. After what felt like hours, she sat up and tried to carefully lift the pillow, planning to put it on the floor.

"If you no longer wish to use the pillow, give me a moment to hop off it first."

She lowered the pillow back into place. Had he still been awake or had the movement woken him? "Never mind. The pillow can stay."

The frog was quiet for a while before he spoke. "What was so important about your golden ball that you were willing to offer so much for someone to fetch it for you?"

It wasn't really any of his business, but it looked like sleep was a long way off. "My mother gave it to me many years ago." She tried to bring the image of her mother to mind, but all she could see was the portrait she'd stared at earlier. "When I was a little girl." She vaguely remembered the moment.

"Where is your mother?"

She remained silent for nearly a minute before she finally answered. "She died, four years and one day ago."

"I'm sorry to hear that. No wonder you were so determined to have your ball returned to you. I'm glad I was able to fetch it for you."

"Does that mean you won't hold me to my promise anymore?"

"Is it such a hardship to have me stay with you?"

He sounded wistful, but that couldn't be right. It was probably a trick of the darkness. "How could you expect me to love you? It doesn't work like that. People can't love on demand."

"Do you feel anything at all?"

She was about to say annoyance. "Gratitude." She owed him that much at least for returning her ball.

The frog made a very humanlike sighing sound. "I suppose that will do for a start."

"Why are you holding me to my promise?"

"I wish I could explain, Princess."

She supposed that meant he had no good reason for it. "How long do you plan to make me keep my promise?"

"Are you wishing me gone already?"

She couldn't resist smiling at the mocking, almost humorous, tone he used. She replied using a similar tone. "Whatever gave you that idea?"

The frog gave a raspy chuckle, but didn't reply.

Calandra remained silent and

eventually drifted off to sleep. When she woke in the morning, her head was on her pillow and she faced the frog, who was awake and staring at her with his protruding eyes. She sat up with a gasp. That was not the best way to wake of a morning. She couldn't stop staring at the frog, wondering what he planned to do next. He returned her gaze, eventually hopping off the bed without a word. Calandra watched him leave her room and she hoped that meant it was the last she'd see of him.

When she'd readied herself for the morning, she made her way to the dining room where she found her father. She glared at him, annoyed that he'd force her to let the frog stay.

Kobus looked around. "Has your guest left already? I would have thought he'd planned to stay far longer.

"I don't know where he's gone or what he plans to do, but I hope he doesn't come back. I can't believe you made me let him stay. And forced me to have him sleep beside me on my bed."

"Mayhap in the future you'll think twice before giving your word."

"Was that what this was all about? Teaching me a lesson? Well I've learned it. Surely now I don't have to let him stay any longer."

Kobus stared at her, slowly shaking his head. "Obviously you haven't learned the lesson." Having finished his meal, he rose from the table and left the room.

Calandra glared at his retreating figure. She had learned it. How could he think otherwise? There was no way she was ever going to promise anyone anything ever again. Or at least not anything she wasn't willing to do.

The rest of the day was uneventful and she didn't see the frog once. She had no idea where he'd disappeared to, but she hoped he didn't return. Her hopes were dashed when he arrived in the dining room that evening.

"Can you put me on the chair beside you, Princess?"

Calandra didn't even bother looking towards her father. She knew there'd be no help there. She picked up the frog and placed him on the chair as quickly as possible. As she sat down in her own chair, she reached for the napkin to wipe her hands clean. Before he asked, she slid her plate closer to him.

"Thank you." The frog helped himself to some of the food on her plate.

Not wanting to go to bed hungry like last night, Calandra picked at the food on the other side of her plate. She tried to think of something to say, the silence at the table unnerving.

"Where do you hail from, Frog?" Kobus asked.

"Please, call me Bastiann."

Calandra stared at the frog. He had a name? Why hadn't he told her? They'd talked for ages last night and not once had he mentioned he had a name.

"Bastiann, where do you hail from?" Kobus asked.

"Several kingdoms away."

"What brought you so far from home?" Kobus asked.

"Curiosity. It has ever been my

downfall." Bastiann turned to Calandra. "Do you mind if we retire? It has been a rather exhausting day for me."

"I suppose not." She rose to her feet wondering if Bastiann really was tired or if he was trying to escape her father's many questions.

Kobus pointed to her plate. "Are you sure you don't want to finish eating first? You've hardly eaten anything tonight."

She started to say she wasn't about to touch the food that was left as it was near what Bastiann had eaten. She glanced towards the frog, changing her mind. "I wasn't very hungry." She turned to Bastiann and helped him down, leading the way to her room. Behind her she could hear him following, the sound familiar.

When they reached her room, she

placed him on the edge of her pillow. Not feeling tired, and with the sun still several hours from setting, she decided to read. She was barely settled in the comfortable chair in the corner of the room when Bastiann crossed the room and asked her to help him onto the arm of the chair.

"I thought you were tired." She sat him beside her, wiping her hands against the skirt of her dress.

"Did you forget our agreement?"

Calandra sighed heavily. "I'm not trying to get out of sleeping beside you. I'm not tired."

"I will sit with you for a while and you can read to me."

She started to argue that it wasn't part of the agreement. Changing her mind she opened the book and began to read. She read to him until the sun was nearly set, marking her place with a length of ribbon and setting the book aside.

"Is that it?" Bastiann asked. "Don't you want to find out what happens?"

Calandra nodded. "Yes, but I can't read out loud anymore." Not without losing her voice.

"Then hold the book for me and I'll read to you."

She stared at him a moment before doing as he asked. It was late by the time they finished the book, having taken turns to read when one grew weary. Without being asked, Calandra carried Bastiann to her bed and placed him on the edge of her pillow.

After putting the lamp out she lay down beside him, careful to remain on her side of the bed since she couldn't see where he was in the dark. "Why did you tell my father that curiosity has always been your downfall?"

Bastiann gave his raspy chuckle. "That is definitely a tale for another day."

"Is that why you wanted to go to bed early? So you didn't have to answer my father's questions?"

He chuckled again. "It sounds like I'm not the only one who has a problem with curiosity."

"How long ago did you leave home?"

"Far too long."

He'd sounded sad, which surprised her. "Why don't you go back?"

"You still trying to get rid of me?"

She smiled at the humour in his tone. "No, at least not deliberately. I really want to know."

"Hopefully one day I'll be able to

return, even if only for a visit. I miss them."

He obviously wasn't going to answer her question. "What are they like?"

She lay awake beside him, talking to him far more than she had the previous night. He told her about his parents he hadn't seen in years and his younger brother he guessed wasn't quite so young anymore. He talked about the last time he'd seen them and shared some of his childhood memories. In return, she shared some of her memories of her mother, more of them coming to mind as she spoke.

As it grew later, she turned on her side, facing his voice. Her words became slower and eventually she drifted off to sleep. When she woke in the morning, she stared at the frog still on the edge of her pillow. He met her gaze. Neither of them moved or spoke for several minutes.

Bastiann turned away and moved to the edge of the bed.

"Where are you going?"

Remaining on the edge of the bed, he faced her. "Still trying to get rid of me?"

She smiled, recognising the humour in his voice. Her smile faded as she realised getting rid of him had been the furthest thing from her mind. "No." She sat up and stared down at him. "You were gone all day yesterday. Will you be gone as long today? Are you coming back this evening?"

"Why? Would you miss me if I didn't return?"

She had no idea how to answer that question. Their long rambling conversation of the night before came to mind. In the dark, she'd forgotten he was a frog. Or if not exactly forgotten, it had become unimportant. "I don't know."

"Exploring."

She was momentarily confused then realised he was answering her earlier question. "Here?"

"To you, this is home. To me, it's a new place. If you were to travel to the next kingdom over, wouldn't you want to explore?"

"Of course." She thought about it for a moment. "I've never been far from home and certainly not out of the kingdom."

"Would you like to travel?"

"It doesn't matter. My father wouldn't allow it."

"What do you want?"

She stared at him while she thought about what it might be like to travel.

"I don't know. How could I when I've never been anywhere else?"

Bastiann talked about distant lands and some of the many things he'd discovered. He spoke of them as if he'd been there and Calandra wondered how a frog had managed to see so many places. She became so caught up in his tales that she lost all sense of time.

A knock on her door startled her. "Enter."

A servant came into her room. "Your Royal Highness, your father sent me to enquire after your health since you haven't left your room all morning."

"Oh, I'm fine." She scrambled off her bed. "Give me a moment to ready myself for the day."

The servant bowed and left, closing the door behind him.

Bastiann hopped off the bed. "I will see you this evening, Princess."

"Calandra."

He gave an awkward nod. "I will see you this evening, Calandra."

As soon as he had left, she dressed for the day and hurried to the dining room, apologising to her father for worrying him.

"What kept you in bed so long this morning? Are you feeling well?"

She nodded. She started to tell him she'd spent the morning listening to Bastiann, but instead said, "I was up late last night reading." A smile curved her lips as she thought of how Bastiann had taken turns reading to her last night.

"You seem in a better mood today. No more glaring at me and trying to get out of your promise?"

"No. I'm sorry. You were right. I

shouldn't have made a promise I wasn't willing to keep."

After they'd finished eating, a footman announced visitors. One of the local nobles and his two daughters had called upon them. Since the girls were similar in age to Calandra, she was expected to entertain them. Their empty chatter and annoying giggles had her wishing she could escape. Maintaining a polite smile and making noncommittal noises she thought of some of the places Bastiann had told her about. Maybe some of them would be worth visiting. She had no idea which ones she would like to see first. They had all sounded so fascinating. Countries edged by the sea, mountains reaching up to the clouds, vast lakes that glittered in the sunlight, sailing a ship through island dotted waters, wandering markets filled with spices and silks and so many other places that she had never known existed.

The rest of the afternoon was taken up daydreaming about distant lands when she should have been paying proper attention to her guests. Sometimes being a princess was tedious. Eventually it was time for their guests to leave and Calandra said goodbye to the girls, trying to sound disappointed their visit was over. She didn't think she was very successful. Hoping Bastiann had already arrived, she headed for the dining room. She was nearly there when a sound had her turning towards the front door.

She could hear the distinctive sound of Bastiann coming up the marble stairs and hurried towards them. She opened the front door as he arrived on the doorstep. "Would you like me to carry you to the dining room?"

"I will be fine, thank you."

She walked beside him. "What did you do today?"

"I discovered all kinds of things. Shall I tell you all about them after we've retired for the night?"

"Is that a promise?" She sent him a sideways glance, a smile almost forming. Bastiann was far more interesting than most of the nobles who called upon them.

Bastiann chuckled. "Yes and I shall honour it."

They reached the dining room and Calandra lifted him and carried him to the seat next to hers. At the same time, she greeted her father who was already seated. Sitting down, Calandra ate her food as quickly as possible. She left her father to carry the conversation, which eventually ended as both her and Bastiann did very little to help.

The moment her plate was empty, Calandra turned to Bastiann. "Would you like me to carry you to my room?"

"If you could put me on the floor I can make my own way there."

Calandra said goodnight to her father, hurrying after Bastiann so she could walk beside him. "What did you do today?"

"If my failing is curiosity, yours would have to be impatience."

"I had a dreadfully tedious day and it was only thinking about the many places you talked of that made it bearable." They reached her room and she opened the door.

"What happened that made it so tedious?"

Picking Bastiann up, she put him on her pillow and sat beside him as she told him about her day. Then she listened as he talked about his day, asking him numerous questions about all he'd discovered. They talked for hours. It was well after the sun had set that they finally lay down to sleep, extinguishing the lamp.

"I've lived around here my entire life and haven't found half the places you've described. How did you manage to find them?"

"Curiosity."

His reply brought laughter to her lips and she was smiling when she fell asleep. The smile was still in place when Calandra woke, slowly opening her eyes. Expecting to see Bastiann on the edge of her pillow, she was shocked to find a young man lying beside her. She sat up, drawing back with a shriek, nearly falling off the edge of her bed.

The young man opened his eyes and smiled. "I thought that was the sound you reserved for frogs."

The voice was so familiar. "Bastiann?"

"Yes." He sat up, continuing to face her.

"What is going on?"

"I was enchanted by a spiteful fairy. He objected to where my curiosity took me and said I'd remain a frog until a princess let me eat from her golden plate and sleep beside her for three nights."

"What about the part where I was meant to love you?"

Bastiann grinned. "I added that the moment I saw you."

Calandra laughed, reaching for

him. "How could I not fall for someone as interesting as you?"

He drew her into his arms. "That's what I was hoping for. Either that or you'd be so entranced by the tales of my adventures you wouldn't be able to resist coming with me, giving you more time to fall in love with me."

"Are you saying you made them all up?" She didn't know whether to be disappointed or more intrigued.

"No, every one of them is true. Including the ones about my family, who I would very much like you to meet."

"That sounds interesting. I wouldn't mind meeting your family after hearing so much about them."

"Is that a promise?" His lips curved into a smile as he continued to meet her gaze.

She couldn't resist returning his

smile. "Absolutely." Her smile widened, becoming a grin. "And I always keep my promises."

Free Ebook

Subscribe to Avril's newsletter and receive a free ebook. This ebook is exclusive to those on her mailing list. To find out more about this offer visit:

www.avrilsabine.com/free-ebook

*

We value your privacy and will not sell, rent, exchange or loan your email address to third parties. Your information is confidential and you are under no obligation to remain on the mailing list and can unsubscribe at any time.

To The Reader

If you enjoyed this book, why not consider leaving a review to help other readers discover it too? Reader engagement is one of the few ways that lets an author know readers want more books in a particular series or genre. So leave a review and tell friends, not only about this book but also about other ones you've enjoyed, so you can continue to enjoy books by your favourite authors for years to come.

Dreams are meant to be lived,
Avril.

About The Author

Avril is an Australian author who lives with her family on acreage in South East Queensland. She writes mostly young adult and children's speculative fiction, but has been known to dabble in other genres. You can find more information about her at www.avrilsabine.com where you can also subscribe to her newsletter to be kept informed about new releases, current projects, blog posts and exclusive news.

Titles By Avril Sabine

Stories about strong characters and characters who discover their strengths.

SERIES

Assassins Of The Dead- Young Adult Fantasy/Paranormal

Book 1: Dark Blade

Book 2: Dragon Touched

Book 3: Society Against Vampires

Book 4: King's Request

Dragon Blood- Young Adult Urban Fantasy (with elements of romance)

(5 book series)

Book 1: Pliethin

Book 2: Wyvern

Book 3: Surety

Book 4: Knight

Book 5: Mage

Dragon Mage- Young Adult Urban Fantasy (with elements of romance)

(Series two of Dragon Blood series)

Book 1: Promise

Dragon Blood Chronicles- Young Adult Urban Fantasy (with elements of romance)

(Companion stand alone series to Dragon Blood)

Book 1: Oath

Book 2: Betrayed

Guardians Of The Round Table- Young Adult Fantasy LitRPG

(Co-written with Storm and Rhys Petersen)

Book 1: Dexterity Fail

Book 2: Goblin Boots

Book 3: Singed Feathers

Book 4: Frog Mage

Book 5: Crystal Mine

Book 6: Cursed Harp

Book 7: Treasure Seeker

Rosie's Rangers- Young Adult Western Steampunk

(6 book series)

Book 1: Justice

Book 2: Vengeance

Book 3: Treachery

Book 4: Accused

Book 5: Wanted

Book 6: Corruption

Mark Of Kings- Children's Fantasy

(Upper middle grade/preteen)

(4 book series)

Book 1: The Arena

Book 2: The Island

Book 3: The Assassin

Book 4: The King

STAND ALONE SERIES

Demon Hunters- Young Adult Urban Fantasy/Horror (with elements of romance)

Book 1: Blood Sacrifice

Book 2: Retribution

Book 3: Tainted

Book 4: Premonition

Book 5: Cursed

Book 6: Feud

Book 7: Extrication

Plea Of The Damned- Young Adult Urban Fantasy/Paranormal

(6 book series)

Book 1: Forgive Me Lucy

Book 2: Forgive Me Aiden

Book 3: Forgive Me Jena

Book 4: Forgive Me Kobe

Book 5: Forgive Me Marti

Book 6: Forgive Me Dawson

Realms Of The Fae- Young Adult Urban Fantasy (with elements of romance)

The Sword (short story in Like A Girl Anthology)

Heart Of Stone

Book 1: A Debt Owed

Book 2: Marked By The Hunt

Book 3: The Magic Collector

Book 4: An Unexpected Betrayal

Book 5: Imprisoned By Iron

Fairytales Retold (Short Stories)

Snow-White And Rose-Red

The Twelve Brothers

The Light Princess

Beauty And The Beast

Sleeping Beauty

Aschenputtel

The Golden Bird

The Frog Prince

The Death Of Koshchei The Deathless

Myths And Legends Retold (Short Stories)

Ion, Son Of Apollo

Sir Gawain And The Maid With The Narrow Sleeves

Princess Ilse, The Giant's Daughter

YOUNG ADULT NOVELS

Young Adult Fantasy (with elements of romance)

Elf Sight

Earth Bound

Young Adult Urban Fantasy

Stone Warrior (with elements of romance)

The Jungle Inside

Young Adult Contemporary (with elements of romance)

Through Your Eyes

The Ugly Stepsister

Perfect Little Princess

Young Adult Contemporary/ Paranormal

Whispers In The Dark (with elements of romance and same sex relationships)

Over Too Soon (with elements of romance)

Young Adult Sci-Fi

Experiment X-One-Six (Urban Sci-Fi/Superheroes)

An Endless Dawn (Post Apocalyptic Sci-Fi)

CHILDREN'S BOOKS

Dragon Lord (Preteen/early teens) (Fantasy)

The Irish Wizard (Upper middle grade) (Urban Fantasy)

SHORT STORIES

Urban Fantasy

Eternally Late

Dealings With Joe

Glimpses (short story in That Moment When Anthology)

Contemporary

The Brat Next Door

Fantasy LitRPG

(Set in the same world as Guardians Of The Round Table Series)

Tales Of Inadon 1: The Disc (Co-written with Storm and Rhys Petersen) (short story in Game On! Anthology)

Post Apocalyptic Sci-Fi

Compulsive Directive

NONFICTION

A Year Of Weekly Writing Exercises (Creative Writing)

Cooking For Families With Allergies (Cooking) (Co-written with Storm Petersen)

Tell Me A Story, Grandma (Memoir)

For the most up to date details on available titles visit:

www.avrilsabine.com/books/bibliography

Disclaimer

This is a work of fiction. Names, characters, businesses, places, events and incidents are either the products of the author's imagination or used in a fictitious manner. Any resemblance to actual persons, living or dead, or actual events is purely coincidental. The opinions expressed or beliefs held are those of the characters and should not be assumed to be the opinions or beliefs of the author.